Owls in the Snow

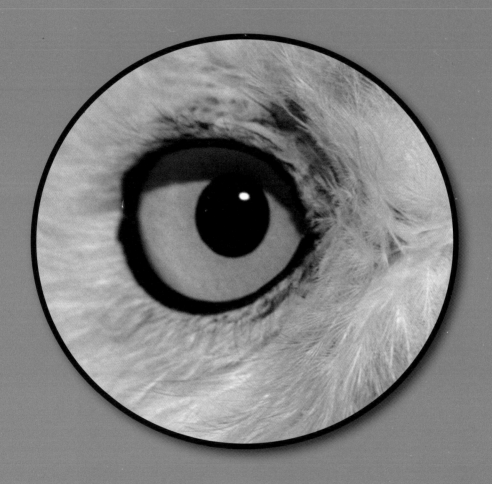

Written by Jo Windsor

Rigby

In this book you will see owls that live in the snow.

You will see...

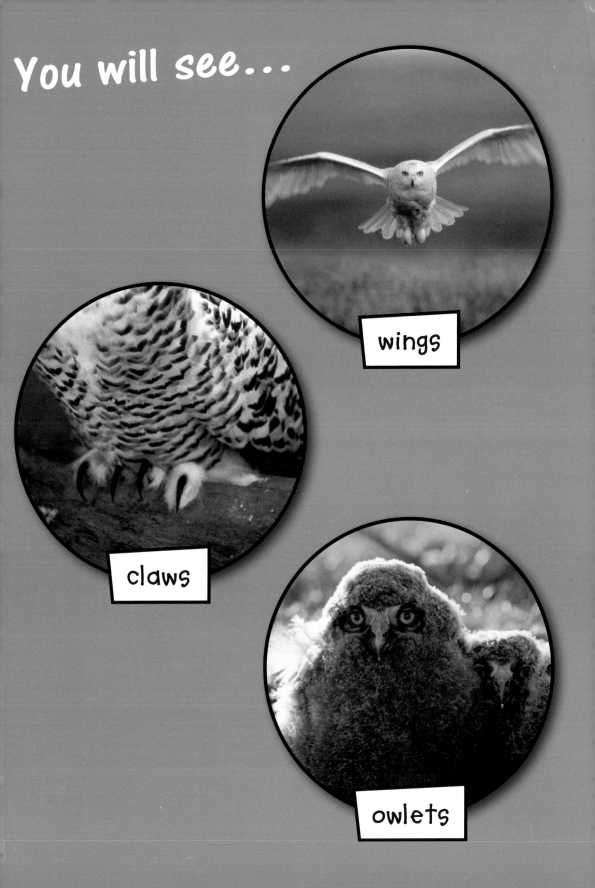

wings

claws

owlets

The snowy owl is a big bird.

It has a big head,
big round yellow eyes,
and a black bill.

bill

A snowy owl lives in a very cold place.

It has lots and lots of feathers
to keep it warm when it is very cold.

It has feathers on its feet
to keep its feet warm, too.

The snowy owl has good eyes.

It is daytime and this snowy owl is looking for food.

It flies over the ground.
Flap, flap, flap go its big white wings.

The owl will get...

apples for food   Yes? No?

grass for food   Yes? No?

animals for food Yes? No?

The snowy owl has big sharp claws on its feet to help get its food.

This snowy owl has an animal in its claws.

claws

A snowy owl eats birds
and small animals for its food.

Sometimes it will get a hare
with its big claws.
And this hare is as big as the owl!

hare

A snowy owl will make a nest on the ground.

The mother bird puts feathers in the nest.

The mother owl lays her eggs in her nest.
The feathers in the nest will help keep the eggs warm.

The eggs will be...

chickens   Yes? No?

owlets   Yes? No?

snakes   Yes? No?

The mother owl stays on the nest.
She will not go away to get food.

If the mother owl goes away,
the eggs will get cold.
The owlets inside the eggs will not live.

How do you think the
baby owls will get food?

The owlets are
coming out of the eggs!

The owlets' eyes
do not open for five days.

They stay in the nest to keep warm.

The nest helps keep
the owlets warm.   Yes? No?

What else will keep
the owlets warm?

The father owl will do all the hunting.

He brings the food back to the nest.
He brings back food for the mother
and the owlets.

Index

Labels

wing

What will go on the owl?

head Yes? No?

hand Yes? No?

hair Yes? No?

feathers Yes? No?

eyes Yes? No?

claws Yes? No?

feet Yes? No?

bill Yes? No?

nose Yes? No?

Word Bank

bill    feathers

claws    head

egg    nest

eyes   wings